MATCH WITS WITH

SHERLOCK HOLMES
Volume 1

MATCH WITS
WITH
SHERLOCK HOLMES

The Adventure of Black Peter

The "Gloria Scott"

adapted by
MURRAY SHAW
from the original stories by Sir Arthur Conan Doyle

illustrated by **GEORGE OVERLIE**

Carolrhoda Books, Inc./Minneapolis

To young mystery lovers everywhere

The author gratefully acknowledges permission granted by Dame Jean Conan Doyle to use the Sherlock Holmes characters and stories created by Sir Arthur Conan Doyle.

This book is available in two editions:
Library binding by Carolrhoda Books, Inc.
Soft cover by First Avenue Editions
241 First Avenue North
Minneapolis, MN 55401

Library of Congress Cataloging-in-Publication Data

Shaw, Murray.
    Match wits with Sherlock Holmes. The Adventure of Black Peter. The "Gloria Scott" / adapted by Murray Shaw from the original stories by Sir Arthur Conan Doyle : illustrated by George Overlie.
        p.   cm. — (Match wits with Sherlock Holmes : v. 1)
    Summary: Presents two adventures of Sherlock Holmes and Dr. Watson, each accompanied by a section identifying the clues mentioned in the story and explaining the reasoning used by Holmes to put the clues together and come up with a solution. Also includes a map highlighting the sites of the mysteries.
    ISBN 0-87614-385-0 (lib. bdg.)
    ISBN 0-87614-528-4 (pbk.)
    1. Children's stories. English. [1. Mystery and detective stories. 2. Literary recreations.] I. Doyle. Arthur Conan. Sir, 1859-1920. II. Overlie, George, ill. III. Title. IV. Series: Shaw, Murray, Match wits with Sherlock Holmes : v. 1.
PZ7.S53426B1   1990
[Fic]—dc20   89-17364
                                                            CIP
                                                            AC
Manufactured in the United States of America

3   4   5   6   7   8   9   10   00   99   98   97   96   95   94   93   92   91

CONTENTS

In the year 1887, Sir Arthur Conan Doyle created two characters who captured the imagination of mystery lovers around the world. They were Sherlock Holmes—the world's greatest fictional detective—and his devoted companion, Dr. John H. Watson. These characters have never grown old. For over a hundred years, they have delighted readers of all ages.

In the Sherlock Holmes stories, the time is always the late 1800s and the setting, Victorian England. Holmes and Watson live in London, on the second floor of 221 Baker Street. When Holmes travels through back alleys and down gaslit streets to solve crimes, Watson is often at his side. After Holmes's cases are complete, Watson records them. These are the stories of their adventures.

INTRODUCTION

Dr. Watson is a retired army surgeon. He is introduced to Sherlock Holmes at a hospital where Holmes is conducting an experiment on bloodstains. Watson quickly sees how extraordinary Holmes is:

"Dr. John Watson, Mr. Sherlock Holmes," said my friend Stamford, introducing us. I held out my hand, and the tall man gripped it strongly. He was lean and wiry, with a thin, hawklike nose and a square chin. His lively dark eyes inspected me.

"How do you do?" he asked me politely. "You are

recently back from Afghanistan, I perceive."

"How on earth did you know that?" I asked, astonished. I wondered if Stamford had told him this.

"I have a turn for observation and deductive reasoning," Holmes said. "And I work as a consulting detective— the only one in the world."

"Do you mean that you can unravel mysteries others cannot?" I inquired, fascinated by his unusual claims.

"Quite so," he said in a matter-of-fact tone. "For example, when I saw you I thought to myself: 'Here is a doctor with a military air. Clearly, he is an army doctor. And his skin is tanned. Thus, he must have been serving in a tropical country as of late.'"

"You are right so far," I admitted.

"Furthermore," said Holmes calmly, "you look weary and hold your arm stiffly, as if you have been injured. So I ask myself: 'Where else could he have seen fighting but in our recent war in Afghanistan?' You see how easily it is done? Observation is the key."

Speechless, I nodded. Never before had I met a person with such highly developed skills in observation and reasoning. I soon discovered that they were skills he practiced constantly.

He would often say, "I see and I observe; others see but they do not observe." Holmes would take the time to look carefully at even the smallest details. Then he would apply all he knew about people's behavior and practical science to reason out answers. And that is how he became a master at his trade, able to solve cases no one else could.

"They were talking when suddenly Carey picked him up and heaved him overboard."

THE ADVENTURE OF
BLACK PETER

The first week in July 1895 had been a busy one for both Holmes and myself. Holmes had been gone quite often, so I knew he was hard at work on a case. During this time, several rough-looking characters appeared at our door, asking to see a Captain Basil. They told me they had been sent by a shipping agent, whose business was to help captains hire crew members. It occurred to me that Holmes might be using the name of Captain Basil to investigate a case, so I told the sailors to call again later.

Then Friday morning after breakfast, Holmes strode into the parlor with a huge barb-headed spear tucked neatly under his arm.

"Good heavens!" I cried. "Have you been carrying that thing all over London?"

"Certainly not, Watson. I took a cab to and from Allardyce's Butcher Shop. Had you been with me, you would have seen me stabbing one of their hanging pigs with this spear. I tried many times, but no matter how hard I tried, I couldn't force this spear through a pig in one blow. And I'm no weakling."

"But what were you trying to prove?" I asked.

"A point in question about the murder at Woodman's Lee," answered Holmes. "After I read the newspaper account last week, I began investigating. Now Inspector Hopkins has wired that he'd like my help. I expect him to arrive at any time now."

Just then a man in his thirties, dressed in a quiet tweed suit, knocked and entered.

"Ah, Inspector Hopkins," said Holmes, "right on time. You know my friend Dr. Watson," he said, gesturing toward me. This was Holmes's signal for me to stay. "Would you care for some breakfast?" he asked the dapper young police officer.

"No, thank you, Mr. Holmes," said the inspector. "I've had mine. What I need is your advice. This is my first big case, and I have made no progress."

"Then, pray, be seated," Holmes said. "I've read the newspaper summary of the Woodman's Lee case, but I'd like to hear Scotland Yard's account."

The inspector nodded and opened his notebook, while Holmes and I settled back in our chairs to listen.

"The facts are these, Mr. Holmes," he began. "Peter Carey was born in '45, and as a young man, he went to sea on a merchant ship. In 1882 he became the successful captain of the Dundee whaling steamer, the *Sea Unicorn*. Carey was a hard-driving captain, and he was called Black Peter because of his thick, black beard and his excessively violent temper."

Holmes filled his pipe as he listened carefully. The inspector continued. "Early in 1884, Captain Carey retired, though he was only thirty-nine. He bought some land at Woodman's Lee in Sussex and settled there with his wife, daughter, and a few servants. Not far from his home, Carey built a small house that looks like a ship's cabin. It has a large built-in bunk and an old sea chest on one end. Next to them is a small table with a picture of Carey's ship hung over it. On the opposite wall is a rack with three weather-beaten harpoons and a small shelf holding a row of worn and frayed logbooks."

Hopkins turned the page of his notebook. "The cabin has a window that faces the road. Two nights before the crime, a stonecutter named Slater passed the cabin on his way home from an evening spent in the local tavern. Slater swears that as he passed the cabin, he saw the dark outline of a bearded man against the curtain of the lighted window. He insists that it wasn't Carey he saw. Carey had a full, bushy beard, and he claims this man had a short beard that stuck directly out from his chin."

"This occurrence, though, may not have any connection with the murder," Hopkins added. "The cabin is a distance from the road, and Slater's tavern friends say that his story should be taken with some caution. He was drinking heavily that night."

"I understand perfectly," said Holmes.

The inspector leaned forward in his chair, his voice getting lower. "Late on the night of his terrible death, Carey staggered to his cabin. He had been angry and dangerous all day. Sometime in the middle of that night, his daughter was abruptly awakened by a piercing cry.

But she was used to her father's rages, so she went back to sleep and thought no more about it.

"The next morning one of the maids noticed the cabin door was open. She approached and peered in. Then she went off screaming, and I was sent for." Hopkins took a long breath.

"Gentlemen," he said, "I have steady nerves, but no soldier's training could have prepared me for the sight in that cabin. Blood was splattered over everything, and the captain was pinned to the wall with a harpoon. The weapon had been driven with such force that it went directly through his chest and into the wall behind him with one stroke. And at his feet lay his knife, still in its sheath."

The inspector fumbled with his notebook, clearly upset. Holmes, on the other hand, was the picture of relaxation, calmly puffing on his pipe.

"Was there any sign of robbery?" asked Holmes.

"No, sir," answered Hopkins. "But Carey was fully dressed, and on the table lay two dirty glasses and an empty bottle of rum."

"Anything else?"

"Nothing of importance, except the captain's tobacco pouch. It's made of sealskin and has the initials P. C. on its cover. Although Carey smoked very little, he must have kept this tobacco for friends. It has half an ounce of strong ship's tobacco in it."

"And what do you make of these clues?" Holmes asked, gesturing with his pipe.

"It is my thought that the captain waited up for his

visitor," Inspector Hopkins replied. "After drinking together, the two of them began to fight. The killer took one of the harpoons from the rack and stuck the captain to the wall. The killer must not have planned to murder Carey, or he would have brought his own weapon. That is, of course, unless he had already visited the captain earlier and knew about the harpoons."

Hopkins was watching Holmes carefully for his reaction. Having finished smoking, Holmes knocked the used tobacco from his pipe into an ash container. "Yet you found no pipe in the cabin," he said. "I find that odd; don't you?"

"Yes," Hopkins stammered, "it is." Then the inspector reached into his coat pocket and drew out a small notebook with a bloodstained cover.

"This is the one piece of evidence not mentioned in the newspaper report," Hopkins stated.

Holmes examined the notebook. Handwritten on the first page were the initials *J. H. N.* and the year *1883*. On the pages that followed were headings, such as *C. P. R., ARGENTINA,* and *AUSTRALIA.* Beneath each heading was a list of numbers or company names.

"It appears," said Holmes, "to be a list of stock and bond investments in foreign companies. *C. P. R.* must be Canadian Pacific Railroad. . . . Yet the first page remains mysterious. Who or what is *J. H. N.*?"

Eagerly the inspector spoke up. "It could be the initials of a stockbroker. We're checking for brokers registered at the Stock Exchange during that year. This may be our only real lead to a suspect."

"Ah," said Holmes. "An interesting line of investigation. I'll have to adjust my theory to include this information. Now, was the notebook lying in the blood or splattered with it?"

The inspector thought for a moment. "I believe it was found face down in the blood."

"I see," mused Holmes. "That means the notebook was dropped after the crime was committed."

"The killer must have dropped it as he was leaving," the inspector suggested.

Holmes did not reply. He seemed to be pondering a stubborn clue. Then he said firmly, "Gentlemen, I suggest we take the next train to Woodman's Lee so we can learn more about this matter."

——— ∽ ———

That afternoon, after arriving at the train station in the village of Woodman's Lee, we took a carriage to Carey's house. We were greeted by his wife and daughter. They gave us permission to examine the cabin but refused to come with us.

Taking the well-worn path, we headed through the woods to the one-room cabin. As the inspector bent to insert the key, he paused. Puzzled, he said, "I believe someone has been trying to break in. The wood around the lock is scratched. It wasn't like this when I checked here yesterday."

"We're in luck then," said Holmes. "Whoever did this may return this evening to try again with a better tool. I suggest we be here to greet whomever it is."

During the rest of the afternoon, we inspected the cabin. All traces of the brutal murder were gone. The inspector and I noted nothing suspicious, but Holmes discovered a place on the logbook shelf where it was clear of dust. "It looks like something has been removed," Holmes stated. "It was either a book lying on its side or a small rectangular object such as a box."

———— ✍ ————

That evening we prepared for our unknown visitor. Hopkins suggested we leave the cabin door open, but Holmes felt this would arouse suspicion. "We'll watch from the bushes under the far window," said Holmes, "so we can see what our intruder is looking for."

It was a gloomy task to crouch among the bushes through the sunset and oncoming night. Yet there was a kind of strange thrill to it all—such as a hunter feels. What murderous beast would we meet in the darkness? What raging fight would it take to capture the creature?

A fine drizzle began to fall, and over the sound of the rain on the leaves, we could hear the church bells chime—first midnight, then one o'clock, then two. Each time a villager passed on the road, we would stiffen and wait for approaching steps.

Suddenly, we heard them—steps coming up the path. Then there came the sounds of prying on the lock, a click, and the turning of hinges. A candle was lit in the cabin, and Hopkins moved to the door. We peered through the gauze curtains at the scene inside.

A man about twenty years old stood shivering in the room. He was frail, thin, and so nervous that the candle shook in his quivering hand.

Craning his neck to look around cautiously, he reached over and pulled a ship's logbook from the shelf. For a moment or so, he leafed through its pages. Then he slammed the book shut and replaced it. As he turned to put out the candle, he felt the inspector's grasp upon his neck. The man let out a terrified cry. We left our posts and hurried into the cabin to help Hopkins.

Seeing us rush in, the man sank down on the sea chest, his wide eyes black in the candlelight.

"What are you doing here?" Hopkins demanded. "Tell the truth, or it will go hard with you at the trial."

The frightened young man spoke in a high voice. "My name is John Hopley Neligan, Jr., sir."

Holmes and I glanced at each other. His initials were the ones on the notebook's first page.

"I am here," he went on nervously, "because my father was part of the banking firm Dawson and

Neligan—the one that failed in 1883. When the bank went under, half the families in Cornwall were ruined. My father swore he would pay back all the money the bank owed. He had some investment certificates with a number of prosperous companies, and a bank in Norway offered to buy them. So my father planned a trip to deliver them. He gave my mother a notebook listing all the certificates and how much each was worth. After he left, we heard that a fierce storm came up in the Arctic Ocean along his route. There was never another word from him, and we finally had to accept that he and his small tin box of certificates were at the bottom of the sea." Neligan sighed deeply and looked sadly down at his feet.

"Then a few years ago," he went on, "a family friend discovered that a number of my father's certificates had shown up for sale in London. They had been put on the market by a Captain Peter Carey. I figured the captain must know something about my father if he had the certificates. So I tracked him here.

"By the time I arrived at the village, the captain was dead. But the newspaper report said that the logbooks from his voyages were in the cabin. So I came here last night and tried to get in. The windows and door were locked. Therefore, I returned to the village to get a steel pry and came back to try again this evening."

Neligan put his head in his hands. "But it's just my luck—the logbook pages from the summer of 1883 are missing, the certificates are nowhere in sight, and now you think I'm a murderer. But I'm not, I tell you."

The young inspector scowled at him. "If this is the first time you've been in this room, how did your notebook get here?" he asked. Hopkins took the notebook from his pocket and showed it to Neligan. The young man turned white.

"I was here once before," Neligan admitted, shaking. "I came a week ago, just before sunrise. I wanted to catch the captain early, before others would be around to disturb us. The door was wide open, and flies were swarming all over the place. The cabin was swimming in blood, and the captain..." Neligan swallowed and started again. "The captain was stuck to the wall with a spear through his chest. I'll never get that image out of my mind. My notebook must have fallen from my pocket as I was running away. But I didn't kill him!" His voice had risen to a scream.

Hopkins pulled out his handcuffs. "You'll have your chance to prove that," he said. "But in the meantime, I'm accusing you of the murder of Captain Peter Carey. Get up now. You're going to Scotland Yard." With that, the inspector led him to the door.

———— ✍ ————

On the ride back to London, the train was nearly empty. The rain had stopped, and the countryside was silhouetted by the light from a half moon. Holmes looked thoughtful. "Watson, almost everything points to Neligan, yet I'm still not satisfied," he said. "Did anyone call for a Captain Basil while I was gone?"

Slightly embarrassed I admitted, "Why, yes, Holmes.

Over the last few days, some sailors have called at Baker Street. In all the excitement, they slipped my mind."

He smiled. "Don't worry, Watson. They'll be back. I asked the shipping agent to send me men who are eager to go on an Arctic expedition. Since most of the sailors in town are registered with this company, I expect we'll encounter a wide range of characters."

I laid back in my seat and tried to sleep. I knew better than to question Holmes further. He wasn't going to tell me about his investigative methods until they had proven successful. So now I had one more mystery to ponder—why was Holmes playing the part of Captain Basil, Arctic explorer?

—— ⌇ ——

Early the next morning, two telegrams arrived for Holmes. He opened them eagerly and then broke into a quiet chuckle of satisfaction. He told me briefly of their contents: one was a list of names from a whaling company in Dundee; the other was a brief message from the shipping agent, listing the sailors who would visit Captain Basil the next morning.

"Well, Watson," he said, "I think we'd best invite Hopkins back for breakfast tomorrow. It would be a pity for him to miss the solving of this crime."

—— ⌇ ——

Hopkins arrived promptly at ten o'clock the next morning. A few minutes later, Mrs. Hudson, our land-lady, came to tell us there were three men at the door.

They were waiting downstairs to see a Captain Basil. "Show them in, Mrs. Hudson," Holmes directed, "but one at a time."

As Mrs. Hudson walked to the door, Holmes added in a low voice, "Watson, you would do well to place your revolver at hand." The inspector looked confused by this statement, but Holmes stood straight and calm, his hands behind his back.

The first sailor, James Lancaster, was tall and lanky. Holmes gave him a shilling and dismissed him. The second was a very short and pudgy sailor named Hugh Pattin. He, too, was given a coin and dismissed. The third was a giant of a man—tall, broad-shouldered, and muscular, with a bulldog stance. He stared at Holmes in silence, his bearded chin thrust forward.

"Your name, occupation, and number of sealing voyages?" asked Holmes crisply.

"Patrick Cairns, harpooner, twenty-six voyages, sir."

"Have you your papers?"

The man produced a set of worn papers and handed them to Holmes, who examined them.

"They seem to be in order. Please sign here." Holmes pointed to a paper on the desk. As the man bent to sign, Holmes quickly snapped a pair of handcuffs on his brawny wrists.

Roaring like a maddened bull, the seaman sprang up and wrestled Holmes to the floor, his handcuffed hands at Holmes's neck. Hopkins and I grabbed the man roughly from behind, and I pulled out my revolver. Its cold muzzle against his head quickly convinced the

sailor that further fighting would be useless. We pulled him to a chair and lashed his ankles together with a stiff rope. His huge chest heaved up and down, and his eyes glinted with hate.

Holmes straightened himself out, his eyes cool as ice as he watched Cairns. "Hopkins," he said, "this is your murderer."

"But . . ." Hopkins began.

"Aye," Cairns said fiercely, "I killed him. And I saved others the trouble of doing it themselves. But you can't hang me for murder." The sailor spat out his words, thrusting his shoulders forward.

"Go on," said Holmes.

"Back in '83 I was a harpooner on Black Peter's ship, the *Sea Unicorn*. A sorry excuse for a captain, Carey was, mean and vile. Late that summer we were skimming the Arctic, on hunt for seals, when a storm bore down on us. It was a fierce one, and as we were pumping out the galley, a yacht came up side, signaling for help. A few of us pulled the single sailor out of the boat and onto the deck. He was wet to the bone, but he wouldn't let go of this small box he carried. The captain right away ordered the stranger to his quarters, and we went back to fighting the storm." Cairns's massive wrists strained at the cuffs as he spoke.

"Sometime around midnight, after the storm had broken some, I saw Carey and the stranger near the side rail. They were talking when suddenly Carey picked him up and heaved him overboard. There was a splash and a cry, and I knew he was gone for good. And there was no one to tell the tale but me. Knowing Carey, I kept my tongue. When we shipped in, I changed companies and pulled out on other voyages. Later it came to me that Carey had retired and settled himself at Woodman's Lee. Since I was pressed for money, I thought I should speak to Carey and have him pay me for my silence."

As Cairns spoke we watched him carefully, ready to pounce if he made any move. "We met one night at Carey's cabin," the sailor continued, "and I told him what I knew. At first he tried to bluff out of it, but it didn't work. So he finally agreed to meet me two nights later to make a deal. When I arrived he was vicious as a starving wolf, so I began looking around his cabin for a weapon, just in case. We sat to tip a mug of rum, but I kept my eye on him over the top of my glass. Suddenly, he went for his knife. But he didn't have a chance. Before he could pull it out of its case, I had pulled the harpoon off the wall and drove it into him sharp.... It was him or me," the sailor snarled, daring us to say differently.

"Then I saw the stranger's box on the shelf," he went on, "so I took it. Aye, but my luck was no good from the start. I forgot my tobacco pouch, and the box I took had nothing but paper certificates. I had no use for them. If I sold them, I'd be caught. So I was no better off than before. I thought that I'd best try for a job as a harpooner on the first ship out, and the shippers sent me here." Looking at Holmes with a grimace, he added, "You don't look much like a captain."

"No, I'm not," said Holmes with a note of triumph. "Well, Hopkins, you'll have to retrieve that little tin box and return it to poor Neligan with an apology. Now he can finally clear his father's name."

Hopkins nodded humbly. "Mr. Holmes, you are the master, and I am your humble pupil. I don't know how you did it, but I'm grateful." Taking his prisoner to a waiting cab, Hopkins departed for Scotland Yard.

Now that the case has been solved and the criminal is on his way to Scotland Yard, see if you can figure out how Holmes found the killer. Then check the **CLUES** *to see if you noted all the important details of Holmes's reasoning.*

CLUES
that led to the solution of
The Adventure of Black Peter

After reading about Carey's unusual murder, Holmes reasoned that the killer had to be powerful and skilled with a harpoon. To prove it, Holmes practiced on a dead pig. No matter how hard he tried, he couldn't drive a spear through the pig with one blow. He concluded from this experiment that Neligan was not strong enough or experienced enough to have killed Carey.

The sealskin pouch had the initials *P. C.* printed on it. But Holmes did not assume that it belonged to the captain. Since a pipe was not found in the cabin, Holmes suspected that the pouch could belong to the unidentified killer. And Holmes was right—the killer had the same initials as the man he killed.

Carey quit the sea in 1884 after only a short period as a captain. Holmes suspected that there was an unusual reason for Carey's early retirement. Therefore, he was curious about Carey's life on the ship just prior to his retirement. Since harpooners work on whaling and sealing ships, Holmes figured that the killer was probably a harpooner on the *Sea Unicorn*. So he wired the company in Dundee for the ship's 1883 crew roster. This list of names came in one of the telegrams. Holmes looked down the list and found a harpooner with the initials *P. C.*— Patrick Cairns.

Neligan mentioned that his father's stock and bond certificates had been kept in a small tin box. And it was known that Carey had had the certificates. Holmes suspected, therefore, that the object removed from the logbook shelf was the tin box. He thought it was possible that the murderer knew about the box and took it.

Holmes reasoned that the harpooner who killed Carey would want to leave England as quickly as possible. So, under the name of Captain Basil, Holmes contacted London's main shipping agent and asked for skilled harpooners. He offered high wages and an Arctic escape to draw the murderer out. The shipping company sent Holmes the likely candidates, and once Holmes met Cairns, he knew he had the right man. Cairns was strong and skilled enough to have thrust the harpoon through Carey with one blow, and he had the type of beard Slater described. In addition, Holmes could see on Cairns's papers that Cairns worked with Carey on the *Sea Unicorn* in 1883.

"As we pulled away from the ship, an explosion
went off, and a huge column of fire burst forth."

THE "GLORIA SCOTT"

O ne frosty winter evening, Holmes and I sat in our cozy parlor on either side of a blazing fire. Holmes was sorting some papers.

"Ah, Watson," he said suddenly, handing me a scribbled note, "this would be of interest to you."

I took the crumpled note and read it aloud:

> *The supply of game for London is going steadily up. Head-keeper Hudson, we believe, has now been told to receive all orders for fly-paper and for preservation of your hen-pheasant's life.*

My bewildered expression pleased Holmes. "This note," Holmes said, "struck a man dead with horror when he read it."

"How did this come about?" I asked.

"It's a bit of a story," Holmes replied, sitting back and filling his pipe, "but one that I remember well since it was the first case in which I was ever engaged."

This excited my curiosity. I had tried many times to get Holmes to tell me how he had become interested in the detection of crime. "Do tell, Holmes," I urged.

Holmes smiled and told me the following story:

Watson, you may recall my mentioning Victor Trevor. He was the only friend I made during college. As you know, I am solitary in my habits.

In college I was even more so. One day as I was walking on the chapel green, Trevor's dog came running up and viciously bit my heel. This laid me up for a while. Trevor came to visit me daily until I healed. Being a friendly and outgoing chap, he then invited me to spend the month's vacation with him at his father's estate at Donnithorp. So naturally I did.

The Trevor estate was in the county of Norfolk. It had an old manor house with solid oak beams and brick walls. The woods provided excellent hunting of pheasant and wild duck, and there was good fishing in the stream.

Victor's father, Mr. Trevor, was a stout, burly man of little education or culture. He was a widower who had traveled far and wide and had remembered much of what he had seen. As justice of the peace, he was widely respected for his wisdom and charity.

One evening after dinner, Justice Trevor casually asked me what I could deduce about him from his appearance. Apparently Victor had told him I was clever at deducing information from observations.

"I fear there isn't much," I told him. "I might suggest, however, that you have been going about in fear of being attacked lately."

His smile faded then, and he stared at me in amazement. "Why, that's true. You know, Victor," he said, turning to his son, "there's been a rash of robberies in the neighborhood recently. Our neighbor Turner was attacked and almost killed." Then he asked, "How did you come to such a conclusion, Mr. Holmes?"

His keen blue eyes were watching me suspiciously.

"By your stick," I answered. "From the dated inscription on it, I could see that you've had it just about a year. When I picked it up, I noticed from its weight that you had had lead poured into its head to make it a better weapon."

"That's reasonable," Mr. Trevor said, hesitating slightly. "And do you note anything else?"

"It seems that you've done some digging in your time, judging by your calloused hands," I replied.

"Quite true. I made my money in New Zealand's gold mines." Mr. Trevor was growing increasingly stiff and crisp in his replies, and his gaze more intent.

I continued, "And once you were closely connected to someone whose initials were *J. A.* But later you wished to forget this person."

At this, my dear Watson, he rose slowly to his feet, stared wildly at me, and pitched forward into a dead faint. You can imagine how shocked we were. We quickly poured cold water on his face and wrists.

He opened his eyes. "Boys," he said, "I must apologize for this weakness. There is a slight problem with my heart. It doesn't take much to knock me down." Then he looked at me and said, "I don't know how you managed it, Mr. Holmes, but take it from me—all the detectives in the world would be like children in your hands. Mark my words, sir, this is your life's work. But tell me, how do you know so much about me?"

"It's simplicity itself, Mr. Trevor. Yesterday you pushed up your sleeve to draw the fish into the boat.

At that time I noticed the *J. A.* tattooed on your arm. As the letters are blurred and stained, it seems that you tried to remove them but could not."

"Your eye for observation is certainly keen, Mr. Holmes," said Mr. Trevor in an offhand, careless way. "The mark of a young love can be difficult to lose."

Calm and satisfied in his doubts, the justice sat back to enjoy his cheese and bread pudding. But every so often during my stay, I would catch him looking intently at me, as if measuring my intentions.

One afternoon, while on the garden lawn, a maid arrived with an announcement. A certain Mr. Hudson had come calling to see Mr. Trevor.

"Please show him here," the justice said uneasily.

A small, wrinkled fellow slouched out onto the green. His sea jacket was open at the collar and stained with tar. He smiled with his head at a slant, and his sharp yellowed teeth gave him the look of a weasel.

"It's me, Hudson, sir," he said, presenting himself.

"What are you doing in these parts?" the justice inquired lightly, without showing any enthusiasm.

The stranger's upper lip curled as his smile widened. "I thought you might like to see an old shipmate," he said, leering. "I'm looking for a place to stay."

"I'm sure I can find something for you," Mr. Trevor said slowly. "Go to the kitchen, and you will be given food and drink. Later we'll see about a job."

Hudson bowed his head with false modesty. "Thank you, sir," he said, smirking. "I've fallen on hard times, and I knew I could count on the hospitality of you or your dear friend Mr. Beddoes."

"You know where he is too?" Trevor asked tensely.

"Bless you, sir. I keep track of all my old friends. Fortune has taken good care of all of you." Hudson bowed again and followed the maid to the kitchen.

After the man left, the elder Trevor explained that Hudson had been with him on a ship to Australia. The justice then excused himself. Later we found him stretched out on the sofa in the study, drunk. You can imagine what a surprise this was, my good Watson, for as yet I could detect no reason for his behavior.

In the days that followed, nothing seemed to satisfy Hudson. He was made gardener and then butler's assistant. But still he complained. And he ordered the other servants about as if he owned the place.

Finally, Victor could stand it no longer. He threw Hudson out of the house. But Hudson immediately went to Justice Trevor demanding an apology.

"My boy," said Mr. Trevor meekly to his son, "perhaps you've been a little too hard on Mr. Hudson."

"I've not been hard enough, and neither have you.

This man is the very devil," Victor cried. "We have not had a peaceful hour since his arrival."

At this, Hudson blew up in a rage. "I know when I'm not wanted. I'll go to Beddoes in North Hampton then." And Hudson strode out of the house.

Later we found Mr. Trevor in the study, drunk once more. He apologized for the state we found him in. "Victor," he begged, "you'll not think poorly of your father, now will you?"

Victor murmured, "No, sir," and we quietly exited.

"This is not like him, Holmes," he said softly.

"No, something is clearly bothering him," I agreed. "I think it's best that I leave so things can be sorted out." Victor nodded, and the next day I left.

Well, Watson, less than a week later I received a telegram from Victor, asking me to come back to Donnithorp immediately.

He met me at the station. "My father is dying" were his first words.

"How can that be?" I cried. "Is it his heart?"

"No, it's a kind of stroke," he answered sadly. "The doctor fears he shall not come out of it."

"What brought it on?"

"It's so strange," Victor said, trembling. "This letter arrived by post from Fordingbridge, North Hampton. My father read it and began shaking uncontrollably. Then he fell down, unconscious. Here's the note."

It was at this point, Watson, that I had my first look at this unusual message. As we traveled back to the estate, I tried to find the meaning hidden in it.

Since it was posted in North Hampton and mentioned Hudson, the note was obviously from Beddoes. I tried reading the note backward. But it made no sense. Reading every other word shed no light on the meaning either. Then, in an instant, I could see it. The solution was to read every third word:

> **The** supply of **game** for London **is** going steadily **up.** Head-keeper **Hudson,** we believe, **has** now been **told** to receive **all** orders for **fly**-paper and **for** preservation of **your** hen-pheasant's **life.**

So the real message was: The game is up. Hudson has told all. Fly for your life.

"It's a warning," Victor cried. "What could it mean?"

"It may have something to do with the voyage Hudson and your father took together," I said. "Something criminal must have happened on board."

At this point we reached the tree-lined drive, and Victor gave out a cry of despair. The blinds were drawn on the windows of his house. "We are too late, I fear," he said softly, dropping the reins.

The butler came out to meet us, and he informed us that the master had passed away an hour before we arrived. Justice Trevor had, however, left some documents for his son to read. It was in these papers that we discovered the full story of Justice Trevor's past and why he was so easy on Hudson.

Victor left the papers with me. He didn't want any reminders of his father's death. In these sheets, Watson, all the mysteries hidden in that fatal note are revealed.

*My dear son, now that I am nearing the end
of my life, I feel you should know something of
the life I lived before I settled here. It is a life I
have struggled to keep hidden. Now that Hudson
has arrived, it is no longer possible. As you read
this, I ask you to think gently of your father.*

*It all began when I went into debt and then
stole some money from my employer to pay it
off. I was caught and convicted. Shortly afterward
I found myself a prisoner on the ship the GLORIA
SCOTT with thirty-eight other convicts. We were
being sent to Sydney, Australia.*

*We set sail with a captain, three mates, a
doctor, a chaplain, Lieutenant Martin and his
soldiers, and twenty-six crew members. There
were nearly one hundred men in all.*

*Each prisoner was kept in a small cell, but the
wooden walls were thin and flimsy. In the cell
to my right was a young man who had committed
a crime like mine. His name was Evans. At the
time my name was Jack Armitage, not Trevor.
And in the cell to my left was Tom Prendergast.
He had been put in prison because he had stolen
vast amounts of money from London merchants.*

*Prendergast was a jaunty fellow, energetic and
sure of himself. One day he told me that he had
a friend on board—Wilson, the chaplain. "Wilson's
not a real chaplain," he boasted. "No, siree. He's
come aboard with my money, and he's going to take
care of us right smart. He's bought off most of
the crew and the soldiers," he said. "And in two*

days, we're taking over this ship." Then he paused.

"Are you and your friend Evans with us on this?" he asked me through the wall. "If not, you're against us, and then you're in for trouble."

I knew by the hard edge to Prendergast's voice that this was a deadly warning. Evans and I decided we had to go in on the mutiny. That day Wilson came by with his big black bag to give us what he called "spiritual comfort." He handed each of us a pistol.

Things were going just as Prendergast had said. Then the next morning the doctor made his rounds. When he sat on one of the prisoner's beds, he felt the pistol. The prisoner knew the plot had been discovered, so he tied the doctor up and called out the signal. Wilson came down and let everyone out of their cells, and we rushed to the deck. Prendergast was in the lead, while Evans and I hung behind as best as we could.

Two sentries were shot immediately. Three more soldiers came running—only to be gunned down themselves. Then Prendergast ran to the captain's quarters, pistol cocked. But just as he got there, shots were heard, and Wilson came out smiling. We knew then that the captain was dead.

From there the horror grew. We gathered in the saloon, and Wilson passed out mugs of wine. Many of the prisoners went crazy with their new freedom. Then a thundering noise shook the walls, and the room filled with smoke. When it cleared, Wilson and others lay dead on the floor.

The Lieutenant and some of his men had fired on us through the open skylight. Bellowing in rage, Prendergast and others charged up the stairs. Evans and I slunk off to the side, grateful to be alive. The fight went on, and the convicts easily won. They cruelly killed the few men who remained against them.

After it was over, Evans and I, with six other prisoners, asked Prendergast for permission to leave the ship. We were sickened by all the cold-blooded murdering. Prendergast first theatened to kill us, but then he let us have one longboat, some food, water, a compass, and a map. He thought we'd never survive on the open sea.

As we pulled away from the ship, an explosion went off, and a huge column of fire burst forth. Smoke blanketed everything, and when it drifted off, the GLORIA SCOTT was no more. Pieces of wood were floating all over. Some men were struggling in the water, while others were already dead. Then someone spotted a sailor, badly injured, clinging to a broken mast. The man, as you may already suppose, was Hudson.

We hauled him into the boat, and he told us what had happened. Prendergast had found the ship's first mate sitting on a powder cask with a lighted torch. The mate had threatened to blow the ship up if anyone tried to harm him. Obviously Prendergast had ignored the first mate's warning, and the ship was blown to bits.

After picking up Hudson, we drifted for days

with the currents. Finally, the ship HOTSPUR
spotted us. But before we went aboard, we all
vowed not to tell the fate of the GLORIA SCOTT.
I only tell you now, my son, so you can understand why I fear disgrace.

Luckily, the HOTSPUR took us safely to
Australia. Evans and I changed our names to
Beddoes and Trevor, and started our lives over.
After traveling to New Zealand and working in
the mines, we eventually returned to England. He
settled in North Hampton and I, here. For thirty
years our secret has been kept. But now Hudson
has somehow found us.

The letter breaks there abruptly. Then on the
bottom it begins again in a shaky, barely legible hand:
"All will soon be public knowledge. May God have
mercy on our souls."

"And that, my dear Watson," said Holmes as I
finished reading, "was the end of my first case. Poor
Mr. Trevor didn't live to find out that a police com-
plaint was never filed. Both Beddoes and Hudson
disappeared without a trace. And my dear friend Victor
was so heartbroken he left Donnithorp for good. Those
are the facts of this case, my good doctor, and you
may feel free to use them in your collection."

Now that you have walked through Sherlock Holmes's first
work of criminal detection, check the **Clues** to see if you followed each of his steps. Once you have finished, you'll be ready
to match wits with Sherlock Holmes in his next adventure.

CLUES
that led to the solution of
The "Gloria Scott"

When talking to Mr. Trevor, Holmes suspected the justice was hiding something. Mr. Trevor admitted carrying a stick for protection, and he acted suspicious of Holmes. Taken together, these observations made Holmes wonder what Mr. Trevor was afraid of.

Holmes noticed the initials *J. A.* tattooed on Mr. Trevor's arm. When Holmes mentioned them, Mr. Trevor fainted and then acted very suspiciously. He seemed as if he were trying to hide something. The justice made the excuse that the initials were those of a woman he had once loved, but Holmes was not totally satisfied. Later, when Holmes read the justice's papers, he discovered that J. A. stood for Mr. Trevor's real name—Jack Armitage.

When Hudson arrived and Justice Trevor mentioned that he and Hudson had been shipmates, Holmes began to watch the two of them for clues. Mr. Trevor started to drink and act strangely immediately after Hudson's arrival. Holmes suspected that Hudson had some kind of power over Mr. Trevor. Holmes then wondered if something unusual had happened on the sea voyage they had once shared.

When Holmes read the oddly worded message, he was drawn to the unusual spelling of the words *head-keeper* and *fly-paper*. Since both words are usually without hyphens, Holmes figured this was the key to the hidden message. He made them into separate words: *game*, *keeper*, *fly*, and *paper*. Then he tried to read the message using different word combinations. He found that reading every third word made an understandable message.

Holmes figured that Beddoes and Trevor had agreed upon this three-word code long ago. Mr. Trevor had probably received a coded message from Beddoes earlier that year warning him about Hudson's arrival in England. That was why Mr. Trevor had had the head of his cane filled with lead.